KT-440-171

Jenny and the Jumble Sale

A humorous story
in a familiar setting

First published in 2005 by
Franklin Watts
96 Leonard Street
London
EC2A 4XD

Franklin Watts Australia
45–51 Huntley Street
Alexandria
NSW 2015

Text © Sue Graves 2005
Illustration © Richard Watson 2005

The rights of Sue Graves to be identified as the author
and Richard Watson as the illustrator of this Work have
been asserted in accordance with the Copyright, Designs
and Patents Act, 1988.

All rights reserved. No part of this publication may be
reproduced, stored in a retrieval system, or transmitted
in any form or by any means, electronic, mechanical,
photocopy, recording or otherwise, without the prior
written permission of the copyright owner.

A CIP catalogue record for this book is available
from the British Library.

ISBN 0 7496 5943 2 (hbk)
ISBN 0 7496 5949 1 (pbk)

Series Editor: Jackie Hamley
Series Advisors: Dr Barrie Wade, Dr Hilary Minns
Design: Peter Scoulding

Printed in Hong Kong / China

MORAY COUNCIL LIBRARIES & INFO.SERVICES	
20 14 79 93	
Askews	
JA	

Jenny and the Jumble Sale

Written by
Sue Graves

Illustrated by
Richard Watson

W
FRANKLIN WATTS
LONDON•SYDNEY

Sue Graves

"Going to parties is always lots of fun. But I think the best parties of all are fancy dress parties, don't you?"

Richard Watson

"I hope you enjoy reading the book as much I enjoyed illustrating it!"

Jenny was excited.

She was going to a party.

Party

"It's a fancy dress party," Jenny
said. "But what shall I go as?"

9

"Let's go to the jumble sale," said Granny. "We'll get some good ideas there."

The jumble sale was very busy.

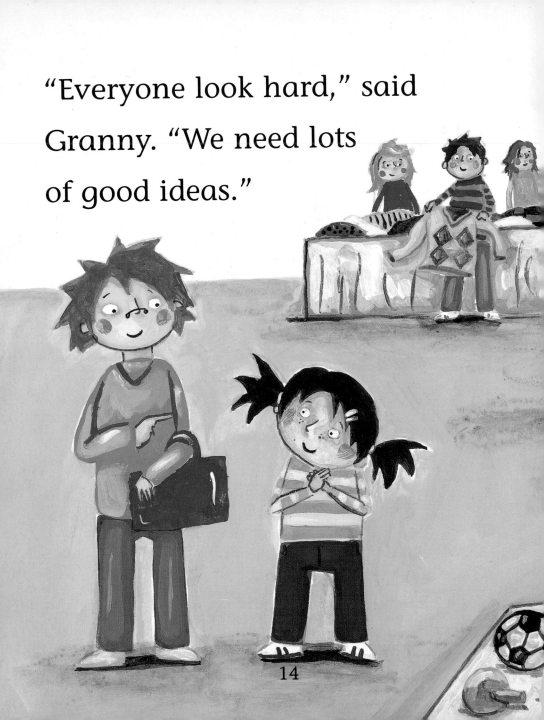

"Everyone look hard," said Granny. "We need lots of good ideas."

Hats

15

Tom found a toy helmet.

Mum found some fairy wings.

18

"You can go as a fairy!" she said.

Dad found a silver suit.

"You can go as an astronaut!"
he said.

Grandad found some flippers
and a mask.

"You can go as a diver!" he said.

Granny found some clown's trousers. "You can go as a clown!" she said.

25

Jenny looked at all the things.
"But which shall I choose?"
she cried. "I like everything!"

27

"You must choose something!"
said Tom.

"I've got an idea," said Jenny.

"I shall go as ...

" ... a jumble sale!"

30

Notes for parents and teachers

READING CORNER has been structured to provide maximum support for new readers. The stories may be used by adults for sharing with young children. Primarily, however, the stories are designed for newly independent readers, whether they are reading these books in bed at night, or in the reading corner at school or in the library.

Starting to read alone can be a daunting prospect. READING CORNER helps by providing visual support and repeating words and phrases, while making reading enjoyable. These books will develop confidence in the new reader, and encourage a love of reading that will last a lifetime!

If you are reading this book with a child, here are a few tips:

1. Make reading fun! Choose a time to read when you and the child are relaxed and have time to share the story.

2. Encourage children to reread the story, and to retell the story in their own words, using the illustrations to remind them what has happened.

3. Give praise! Remember that small mistakes need not always be corrected.

READING CORNER covers three grades of early reading ability, with three levels at each grade. Each level has a certain number of words per story, indicated by the number of bars on the spine of the book, to allow you to choose the right book for a young reader:

GRADE 1	GRADE 2	GRADE 3
50 words	130 words	250 words
70 words	160 words	350 words
100 words	200 words	450 words